The Popcorn Pirates

The Popcorn Pirates

Alexander McCall Smith

illustrations by Ian Bilbey

BLOOMSBURY

This edition published in Great Britain in 2005 by Bloomsbury Publishing Plc,
36 Soho Square, London, W1D 3QY

First published in the UK by Scholastic Ltd, 1999

A CIP record of this book is available from the
British Library

ISBN 0 7475 8054 5

Printed in Great Britain by Clays Ltd, St Ives plc

10 9 8 7 6 5 4 3 2 1

All papers used by Bloomsbury Publishing are natural, recyclable products
made from wood grown in well-managed forests.
The manufacturing processes conform to the environmental
regulations of the country of origin.

www.mccallsmithbooks.co.uk
www.bloomsbury.com

CARIBBEAN SEA

CHAPTER 1

The Popcorn Islands

Have you ever heard of the Popcorn Islands? Probably not. Very few people have – but if you look hard at a map of the Caribbean Sea, you might just see four little dots not far from Jamaica. The dots won't be named, of course – they're too small for that – but those are the Popcorn Islands.

Not long ago, nobody lived on these

islands. From time to time, sailors were shipwrecked on them, and sometimes stayed for months, or even years. Sooner or later, though, they would be rescued and the islands would be deserted again. The shipwrecked sailors were often rather sad to go, as these were comfortable islands, with plenty of fresh water and lots of wild fruit trees. The turtles and birds who lived on the islands were also very friendly, as they hardly ever saw any humans and were always pleased to have some company.

Then, almost one hundred years ago, Lucy's great-grandfather, who was a ship's captain, sailed past the islands and decided to drop anchor and explore them. He liked them a great deal, and his wife, who always went with him on his voyages, liked them even more.

'Let's stay here,' she said to her husband, as they sat on the beach and watched the turtles lumbering up from the water's edge. 'Let's stay here and build a house. I'm tired of sailing around and never staying in one place very long. I want to have a house, with curtains, and sleep in a real bed, with legs, instead of a hammock.'

'I know how you feel, my dear,' mused the captain. 'I'd like to look out of my window and see hills, and trees with birds in them, instead of just waves and more waves.'

'And eat fresh pumpkins,' continued his wife, 'instead of dry biscuits and salted ham.'

The captain spoke to his sailors, and they all agreed that this was a very good idea. They, too, had had enough of pulling sails up and down and singing sea shanties as they climbed the rigging. They wanted to have little houses, with taps that ran fresh water, and plates that didn't always taste of salt when you licked them. So they left the captain and his wife and took the ship off and fetched their own wives and children. Then they returned to set up home on the Popcorn Islands. And that is how it all started. It was as simple as that.

As the years went by, the number of people on the islands grew. By the time that Lucy's grandfather was born, there were fifty people on each of the four islands, and by the time that Lucy herself arrived, there were one hundred and twenty-five people on each. And that was about right, as it meant that there were just enough people for everybody to be able to find friends, and not so many that the islands became crowded.

It was Lucy's grandfather who made the great discovery that was to give the islands their name. In his day, they had no real name, and were simply called Big Island, Middle Island, Small Island, and Tiny Island. Then one day, when he was wondering whether he would plant pumpkins and melons again that year, he made the amazing discovery that the soil of the islands was suitable for growing popcorn. In fact, it was perfect for it. If you put some popcorn under a shallow covering of the islands' rich, dark soil, within a few days a strong little popcorn plant would be pushing its way up into the light.

Then, less than six weeks later, you would have a lush crop of popcorn ripening in the sun, ready to be picked.

It was a marvellous discovery and everybody was quite overjoyed.

'It will be a great change from growing pumpkins,' people said. 'Imagine having all the popcorn we could possibly want, right here on our doorsteps!'

'And we can sell it too,' said another. 'We can send it off to America by boat. They love popcorn there!'

'We'll all become rich!' said another. 'Fancy that!'

Well, not everybody became rich, but certainly they did very well out of popcorn, and soon there was a thriving trade. From then on, it seemed natural to call the islands the Popcorn Islands. It suited them so well, and the people were proud to come from a place with a name like that.

They were, not at all surprisingly, all very happy – until things suddenly went very badly wrong.

CHAPTER 2

The Popcorn Ship Arrives

Lucy lived on one of the popcorn plantations on Big Island. She had a brother, Sam, who was a couple of years younger than she was, and a friend, Hermione, who lived on the neighbouring plantation. She and Hermione spent most of their time together, and even at night they could send messages to one another by torch. All you had to do was to stand at your bedroom window and flash the message out across the darkness of the popcorn fields. Then the answer would come back through the night: *flash, flash, flash!*

During the popcorn-picking season, the island school was closed. This allowed all the children to play their part in bringing in the harvest, which was something everybody had to do. Even the island teacher and the island policeman had to lend a hand. And at the end of it all, when the popcorn crop was safely harvested, everybody had a wonderful party on the beach, with people singing the old popcorn-picking songs and eating as much of everything as they could possibly manage.

There were dancing competitions, too, and Sam always did very well at these. He was double-jointed, which meant that he could dance under a pole which was only a couple of hands' widths above the ground. Everybody enjoyed watching Sam show just how bendy his bones were and they clapped and cheered when he finished his per-formance.

The next day, the popcorn ship was due to arrive. This ship came without fail the day after the harvest was completed and everybody would go down to the harbour to welcome it. Captain Foster, who owned the ship, was very popular on the island as he always allowed the children to come aboard and drink the special lemonade that he made for them. It tasted like no other lemonade, and everybody was allowed to drink as much of it as they wanted.

Captain Foster had a dog, Biscuit, who was also very popular with the children. He was not a very large dog, and he walked in a very peculiar way, sideways rather than forwards. Yet he was very friendly, and would bark with delight when any of the children came on board.

Lucy was one of the first to welcome Captain Foster on that particular day. She and Sam

ran down to the harbour and were soon
joined on board by Hermione. They gave
chocolate drops to Biscuit, who could not
resist them, and chatted to Captain Foster

while they drank their lemonade. Then, when everybody had had enough lemonade, the serious business of loading the popcorn began.

The loading of the popcorn usually took the whole day, and again everybody had to lend a hand. Then, when the last sack had been put into the hold and the hatches lowered into place, everybody went ashore to wave farewell to Captain Foster and Biscuit. The captain did not like to spend too long in the harbour, as he had a long way to sail with his cargo of popcorn and he knew that he would have to return straight away to get the second half of the crop.

Lucy and Hermione ran down to the beach near the harbour and waved to Captain Foster as the popcorn ship sailed out into the open sea. Then, when it was no more than a dot on the horizon, they went home.

That night, Lucy flashed a message through the darkness.

'When do you think Captain Foster will be back?' she asked, in the special code that they had invented.

Flash, double flash, flash, flash, came the reply, which meant, 'I think he'll be back next Sunday, although he might make it by Saturday.'

Lucy thought that it might be Monday, as she had heard that there were storms at sea and these might hold Captain Foster up. They were both to be proved wrong. The next day, as Lucy was sitting reading in her room, she heard her brother shout from his tree house in the garden.

'The popcorn ship!' yelled Sam. 'Look! Captain Foster's back!'

Lucy ran outside to see if her brother was imagining things. But he was not: for there, coming into the harbour, was the unmistakable shape of the popcorn ship. Captain Foster had returned already!

Lucy ran down to the harbour, to find Hermione waiting for her. Then, when the ship had tied up, she and her friend rushed aboard to find out what was wrong. They found Captain Foster on the front deck, and they could tell immediately that there was something very seriously wrong. Even Biscuit, who normally barked a welcome to the girls, was silent, his head lowered, his tail drooping sadly between his legs.

'We've been robbed,' said Captain Foster miserably. 'Every last sack has been taken.'

Lucy glanced towards the hold. The hatches were wide open, and there was clearly nothing at all inside.

'Who robbed you?' she asked. 'How did it happen?'

Captain Foster sighed. 'Pirates,' he said. 'They found me just about four hours off the island and they came aboard. They took everything, even Biscuit's dog food.'

Lucy and Hermione gasped. Pirates! They had heard of pirates, of course, as everybody had, but were there still pirates on the prowl, even today? Somehow they seemed to belong to the history books, when people really feared the Jolly Roger flying from the mast. Surely that sort of thing didn't happen any longer?

It was as if Captain Foster could read their thoughts.

'Yes,' he said. 'I know that everybody thinks that pirates are a thing of the past, but they still exist, believe me! They aren't quite so bad as they used to be, I suppose, but they're still pretty wicked. In the old days they would have made me and Biscuit walk the plank – at least they didn't do that!'

Later, in the kitchen of Lucy's house, over a bowl of soup which Lucy's mother had prepared for him, Captain Foster told everybody what had happened.

'The first I knew of it,' he said, 'was when I saw a ship in the distance. I didn't think much of it, as there are quite a few ships sailing about out there, but there was something about this one which soon made

me take notice. She was sailing straight towards me, you see.

'I thought at first that she might be in trouble. We sailors help one another out, you know, and so I stopped my engine and stayed where I was. In a few minutes they were up alongside me and I saw that they were a large sailing ship, with great white sails and a long pole at the prow. It was a beautiful ship, really, and I suppose that is why I didn't notice at first that there was a black flag fluttering from the foremast.

'They came up beside me and threw a rope across. Then, when they were close enough, a couple of men jumped aboard. I was beginning to worry a little bit now, because these men did not look in the slightest bit friendly, and I could tell that they clearly needed no help from me.

'Biscuit didn't like the look of them either, because he gave a growl and then a loud bark. One of the men looked at him, and then gave him a good kick, sending him shooting across the deck.

'"Don't you treat my dog like that!" I shouted angrily.

'"You keep quiet!" said one of the men fiercely, drawing a knife from his belt. "You just open your hatch for us."

'I realised that I had no choice but to do what they ordered, and so I opened the hatch and had to stand and watch while they unloaded every single sack of popcorn and tossed it over into their own ship. Then, when they had finished, they got a piece of rope and tied me to the mast. They thought this was very funny, and they laughed as they jumped back on to their own ship and sailed away.

'I was in a spot of bother. As you know, my ship is a single-handed one and there was nobody there to help me. We could drift for days like that, and even run into rocks somewhere. So I more or less gave up any hope of being saved.

'I had forgotten about Biscuit – as had the pirates. No sooner was their ship out of sight than he bounded up to me and started to tug away at the rope with his teeth. It took him some time, but at last he did it, and I was loose. So I turned round and came straight back here to tell you all about it.'

'Thank goodness for Biscuit,' said Lucy. 'Without him . . .'

'Yes,' said Captain Foster. 'He saved my life.'

'But what are we going to do now?' asked Lucy's father. 'What are we going to do about the rest of the popcorn? Surely you won't want to set sail with it tomorrow. Those pirates could still be lurking out there somewhere.'

Captain Foster thought for a moment. There was clearly a risk that the pirates would return, but he couldn't stay on the island for ever. They had to get the popcorn off to market somehow, and if *he* didn't take it, then who would?

'I'll have to set sail again tomorrow,' he said. 'I really don't think there's anything else I can do.'

CHAPTER 3

Hermione Has an Idea

That night, Lucy lay in her bed and thought about Captain Foster's plight. It would be only too easy for the pirates to raid his ship again, and if that happened there would be no popcorn at all to sell. How would people live if they couldn't sell any popcorn? Everybody would go hungry, she thought, and have to live on pumpkins. The thought made her shudder. Pumpkins for breakfast, lunch and supper – for months on end! And pumpkin sandwiches at school as well!

She got out of bed and went to her window. It was completely dark, and even the sea-grape tree outside her window was no more than a large black shape. She looked in the direction of Hermione's house, out across the fields. Would her friend still be awake, she wondered. Was she also wondering what to do?

Lucy got her torch out of her cupboard and returned to the window. Then, pointing the torch out into the darkness, she flashed her signal.

'Are you still awake?' she asked.

For a few moments nothing happened, and Lucy decided that Hermione must be asleep. But then, through the darkness, a pinpoint of light flashed out.

'Yes. I've been lying here thinking. I'm so worried about Captain Foster and the pirates that I can't go to sleep.'

'So am I,' replied Lucy. 'Surely there's something we could do.'

Flash, flash-flash, double flash, flash, flash, went Hermione, which meant, 'Perhaps we could go with him. We could keep a lookout for the pirates while he sails the ship.'

Lucy thought for a moment before she replied. 'But what if we see them? What then?'

Hermione's answer came back through the darkness. 'If we see them in time, then we'd have a good chance of getting away. Captain Foster's ship's quite fast.'

Lucy was not sure about this plan, but it seemed to her that unless anybody came up with a better idea, it was worth trying.

'Let's tell them about it tomorrow morning,' she signalled back.

'Yes,' flashed Hermione. 'Good night.'

Lucy went back to bed. Hermione was well known for having good ideas, but Lucy was not so sure about this one. Still, she

thought, even a bad plan is better than no plan at all.

The next morning, Hermione arrived at Lucy's house well before the rest of the household was out of bed. She and Lucy discussed their plan, before revealing it at the breakfast table to Captain Foster and Lucy's parents.

'Would it help if you had some warning of the pirates?' Lucy asked the captain, as he put marmalade on his toast.

'Yes, I'm sure it would,' replied Captain Foster. 'But when it's just you sailing a ship you don't have time to keep a lookout. And you've also got to stop the ship to get some sleep, you know. And then there's nobody to see what's happening.'

Lucy glanced at Hermione, who nodded encouragingly.

'We'll be your lookouts,' said Lucy. 'Hermione and I have discussed it, and we'd like to come along.'

'With me!' said Sam, who had been listening to all this with interest. Nobody had asked him, but he was determined that he would not be left out.

'Oh, I couldn't,' said Captain Foster. 'It's far too dangerous.'

'But we'd be able to get away from the pirates,' Lucy said. 'You said that they only had a sailing ship. You've got an engine on your ship.'

Captain Foster stroked his beard and looked at Lucy's parents, who were whispering quietly to one another.

'We'll let them go,' said Lucy's father. 'That popcorn simply has to get through. If the children can help, then I think we should let them. It's a pity we can't go ourselves – we're far too busy planting.'

Captain Foster still looked doubtful, but he realised that there really might be no other way, and so eventually he agreed. Now all that remained to be done was to ask Hermione's parents, and they, when they heard what was planned, agreed to let her go.

'Remember your toothbrush, though,' said Hermione's mother, who tended to fuss a bit. 'And if you do see any pirates, I don't want you to pick up any rough manners from them. Do you understand?'

There was not much time left for preparations. While everybody else helped to load the popcorn on to the ship, the three children packed their bags and made sure that they had everything they needed. Hermione's father spent the whole day making pies for the voyage, and Lucy's mother, who was the quickest sewer on the island, made three splendid sailor suits for the children to wear.

Then, when everything was ready, Lucy, Hermione, and Sam set off for the harbour, wearing their new sailors' outfits and carrying their bags of provisions.

'Welcome aboard!' said Captain Foster from the top of the gangway. Biscuit, who was standing beside him and who was very pleased at the prospect of more company on the voyage, gave a loud bark of delight.

The whole island had turned out to wave them goodbye, and as the ship slipped out of the harbour, the three children stood on the deck and waved and waved until their arms could wave no longer. The people on the shore were smaller now, and soon they were no more than dots.

Lucy looked at Hermione. Her friend was always very brave, and this made her feel brave too, but now, as they faced the open sea the thought of pirates made her shiver.

'I hope we don't see the pirates,' she confessed to her friend. 'I'm a little bit scared.'

Hermione smiled. 'So am I,' she whispered back. 'But let's try not to show it! We wouldn't want Sam to know.'

Sam, who was standing next to Biscuit, turned and whispered into the dog's ear.

'I'm rather frightened, Biscuit,' he said under his breath. 'But please don't tell the girls.'

Biscuit wagged his tail and gave a bark. He wasn't in the slightest bit afraid of pirates, and if they showed their faces around the popcorn ship again, they were going to get a very nasty surprise from him!

CHAPTER 4

Unwelcome Visitors

They had set sail in the mid-afternoon and by the time they lost sight of land it was almost sunset. They had had a busy few hours, unpacking their bags and slinging up their hammocks down below, and now Captain Foster was telling them their duties.

'The night is divided into watches,' he said. 'A watch will be four hours long and you'll have one watch each. You'll start, Sam, because you're the youngest, and then it'll be Lucy and Hermione, one after the other. That'll take us through to morning.'

'What do we do?' asked Sam. 'Do we steer the ship?'

'No,' said Captain Foster. 'I'll put down the sea anchor later on and we'll switch off the engine. So all you'll have to do is keep a good lookout for any other ship. If you see anything, come down and wake me up.'

'It could be pirates, you see,' explained Hermione, making everybody shiver slightly as she mentioned the word.

Sam nodded. If there were going to be pirates, he very much hoped that they would come in somebody else's watch.

They had dinner together, eating two of the pies which Lucy's father had made. It was dark now, and everybody felt lonely and far from home. The sea around them was gentle, with only the smallest of waves, and the sky above was a great dome of stars. You feel bigger on land, thought Lucy. Out here you feel very, very small.

The best place for the watch was right at the front of the ship. Sitting there in the darkness, one would see the lights of any approaching ship and there would be plenty of time to wake Captain Foster. Sam felt very nervous during his watch, but nothing happened while he was up there and eventually the time came for him to go off to wake his sister. He felt very proud of himself, and very pleased that his duties were over.

Lucy took some time to wake up, but eventually she struggled out of her hammock and made her way up on deck. The hours seemed to pass very slowly, but at last she, too, was finished, and it was Hermione's turn.

Nothing at all happened that night, and the children were beginning to feel a bit more confident by the time that Captain Foster got up and started the engines again. Soon they were ploughing through the sea once more, with a fresh wind behind them helping them on their way, and wonderful-smelling breakfast sizzling away on the cooker.

After breakfast, they again took it in turns to sit up on the top and keep a lookout. Other ships were sighted now, but each time that Captain Foster was called he looked through his telescope and shook his head.

'Banana boat on the way from Barbados,' he would say. Or, 'Pleasure yacht from Florida, going over to the Caymans.'

There was no sign of the pirates, and everybody began to think that the last time they had struck it had simply been bad luck. Perhaps that was the last they had heard from them, and the pirates would just be a bad memory.

Then, shortly after lunch, while Sam was keeping lookout, he gave an excited shout.

'Captain!' he called. 'A ship off to starboard, coming our way, I think!'

Captain Foster came out of the wheel-house and put his telescope to his right eye. Lucy and Hermione strained their eyes to see, too, but the ship was too far away and it still looked no more than a black smudge on the horizon.

Captain Foster lowered his telescope and frowned.

'I don't like the look of that,' he said. 'I can't be certain – it's still a bit far away – but I'm going to increase our speed a little and change our course by a few degrees. You keep a very close watch on her, will you?'

He passed the telescope to Lucy and pointed in the direction of the distant ship.

'Let me know the moment she does anything unusual,' he said. 'I'll be in the wheelhouse.'

Lucy took the telescope and trained it on the other ship. She could make out a bit more now, but it was still very far away. As she did so, she heard the note of the ship's engine change slightly as Captain Foster increased speed.

For the next fifteen minutes, the children kept an eye on the distant ship. It seemed to be on the same course as themselves, they thought, and very slowly it was getting closer. They were now able to make out its masts, and at one point Lucy thought that she could see one or two people on the deck.

'Go and tell Captain Foster that it's following us,' Lucy said to Sam.

Sam passed on the message and Captain Foster came up on deck and took the telescope from Lucy. He studied the other ship for a few moments, and then lowered the telescope.

'It's them,' he said. 'I recognise their ship!'

'Can't we go any faster?' asked Hermione. 'Can't we just sail away from them?'

Captain Foster sighed. 'I'm going full speed as it is,' he said. 'But they've got a pretty stiff wind behind them and they're gaining ground.'

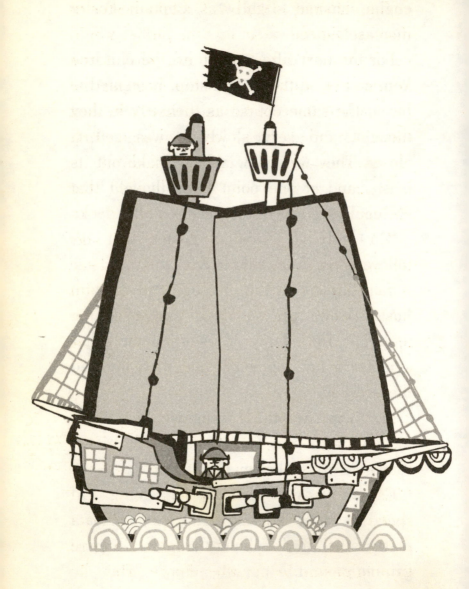

The children looked at Captain Foster in dismay. Did this mean that the pirates would catch them? And if they did, what then? Would they all be tied to the mast, as the pirates had done to Captain Foster the last time? Or might they even change their minds and make them walk the plank?

Captain Foster saw how worried the children were, and he tried to reassure them.

'We're not beaten yet,' he said. 'You stay up here. I'm going to go down below and see if I can tinker with the engines to get a bit more speed. Lucy, just take the wheel for me, will you?'

Ten minutes later, Captain Foster came up on deck again. The pirate ship was a bit closer now, and it was possible to make out the rigging on its high masts and see the distant fluttering of its black flag. Captain Foster looked at the approaching ship and herded the children into the wheelhouse. Then he addressed them gravely, as a captain might before his ship goes down.

'It looks as if they're going to catch us,' he said. 'I have a duty to make sure that you people are not harmed. So what you are going to do is hide, all three of you, and Biscuit too. I don't want him making any trouble with the pirates.'

'But what about you?' asked Lucy. 'We can't just let you face them alone.'

'It will be far better that way,' said Captain Foster. 'They'll take the popcorn and then they'll probably tie me up, the same as before. But once they've got back on to their ship, you can come out and set me free. It's the best thing to do, as far as I can see.'

The children had to agree, although they all felt that they were rather letting Captain Foster down. He showed them to their hiding place, which was at the back of the wheelhouse, under a pile of old popcorn sacks. If they stayed quite still, then none of the pirates would dream of looking in a dusty old pile of sacking. They should be perfectly safe.

'Right,' said Captain Foster briskly. 'In you get. Stay absolutely quiet and don't make any movements, whatever happens. And if anybody wants to do any sneezing, you'd better do it now!'

Lucy and Hermione fitted under one sack, and Sam and Biscuit under another. Then Captain Foster stood back and checked to see that they were properly hidden.

'Good work,' he said. 'Now remember what I said about staying still.'

The children did not have long to wait. Ten minutes later they heard a shout from above and a jolt ran through the ship.

'They're coming aboard,' whispered Hermione. 'The pirates are here!'

CHAPTER 5

Biscuit's Mistake

It was difficult trying to keep still under those old popcorn sacks. Lucy's legs were in an uncomfortable position and she would have loved to be able to stretch them, but she couldn't, of course. For Hermione, the worst part about it was not being able to see what was happening. If only she had had a little hole in the sacking to peer through, she would have felt much better. There's nothing worse, she thought, than being hidden and not knowing whether somebody is standing right next to you, or even looking down at you, wondering what those peculiar shapes under the sacking might be.

And as for Sam, he was busy trying to keep Biscuit still. The little dog had started off being quite happy under the sacks, but now he was showing signs of having had enough of this peculiar game and wanting to get out. So Sam had to stroke him and tickle him under his hairy chin to keep him amused.

After some time, the sound of thumping and bumping from the hold came to an end. The sacks must now have been unloaded, and, with any luck, the pirates might sail away.

'Only a few more minutes,' Lucy whispered to Hermione. 'Then we can get out and –'

She was interrupted by the sound of

footsteps. They heard the door of the wheelhouse open and there were voices.

'So where do you keep your money?' asked a rough voice.

'There isn't very much,' came Captain Foster's voice. 'I keep telling you that. Anyway, it's not here – it's down below. There's nothing in here for you.'

'Oh, yes?' came another voice, a cruel, horrible voice that sent shivers down the spine. 'You seem very keen to keep us out of the wheelhouse, doesn't he, Bert? So what are you hiding in here?'

'Nothing,' said Captain Foster quickly. 'Nothing at all.'

'We'll be the judge of that,' said the first voice. 'I think that we might take a little look round, just to be sure. What do you think, Stinger?'

The pirate called Stinger grunted his agreement.

'Why not, Bert? You never know your luck. That's what I always say.'

Lucy reached out and gripped Hermione's hand. This is the end, she thought – they're bound to find us.

They felt the vibration of footsteps through the planks of the deck. Then they stopped.

'What's in those sacks?' asked Bert.

'Nothing,' said Captain Foster, his voice almost breaking with fear. 'They're just old popcorn sacks.'

Bert snorted. 'You should keep your ship tidier,' he said. 'Just like us.'

Then Stinger spoke. 'Come on, Bert,' he said. 'We can't spend all day here. Let's go.'

And at that point, Biscuit barked.

You couldn't really blame Biscuit. He had been very good until then, but at last it was just too much for a dog to bear, and he barked. He had recognised the voice of one of the pirates, and he was filled with indignation. How dare these people come back on to his ship? No self-respecting dog would allow them to get away with it.

'Ah!' shouted Stinger. 'I suppose you'll be

telling us that that's the ship's cat! Well, let's just take a look.'

The sack covering Sam was torn off and the boy and the dog were exposed. Then, with a deft flick of the wrist, Stinger pulled the sacking off Lucy and Hermione, and they, too, were revealed, crouched on the floor.

'Ah ha!' crowed Bert. 'So, what have we here? Are these stowaways, my good captain, or was you just lying to us all along?'

'Just leave them alone,' said the captain. 'You've got what you came for. Now just leave us alone.'

Bert shook his head.

'Oh no,' he said. 'I think that we might go away with rather more than we'd expected. What do you think?'

He turned to Stinger, who was a mean-looking man with a narrow face and lips that curled downwards in a constant snarl.

'We could do with a couple of extra hands

in the galley,' he said, pointing to Lucy and Hermione. 'And as for that young man, he'd do fine for climbing up to the topsail. Boys like that can get places we can't get. They likes high rigging!'

'Good idea,' said Bert. 'Now let's just tie up the good captain here. We don't want him getting any funny ideas about chasing us, does we?'

The children were powerless to help and Captain Foster, who did not want to do anything which could endanger the children, had no choice but to allow himself to be securely tied to his chair in the wheelhouse. Then, with a shout to the other pirates, Bert and Stinger led the children off to the side of the ship and tossed them, as if they were sacks of popcorn, on to the deck of the waiting pirate vessel.

The children huddled together miserably on the deck while the pirates busied themselves with getting their ship under sail. Then, when they were on their way, and

pulling away from the sad sight of the drifting popcorn ship, the children were led by Stinger to Bert's cabin. Bert, it appeared, was the chief of the pirates, and he had the best cabin on board.

'Right,' said Bert, in a business-like voice, pointing to Lucy. 'You two girls are to report to the galley. You tell Mrs Bert that you're her assistants. It's your new job. Now, let me see, what about pay? You always gets told your pay when you gets a new job. So, what are you landlubbers worth, eh? Ten hours work a day, at . . . oooh, nothing an hour, makes . . .'

'Nothing, boss,' said Stinger, laughing.

'Well done, Stinger,' said Bert. 'You was always very good at arithmetic. Pity you're so stupid at everything else.'

Stinger laughed.

'You're the one with the brains, Bert,' he said cheerfully. 'I always knew that.'

'Thank you, Stinger,' said Bert. 'That's how I got where I am today. Brains. There's no substitute for brains, I say.'

He turned to Sam, whose knees were knocking with fear, although he hoped it didn't show.

'Now you, young man. What's we got for you? Got a head for heights, have you? I hope so, because if you hasn't, then I'm afraid you're going to fall in. And pirate ships never goes back. If a man falls in, then it's the sharks for him, I'm sorry to say. I've seen many a man eaten by sharks, hasn't I, Stinger?'

'Oh, yes,' said Stinger, smiling at the thought. 'Old shark likes nothing better than a boy for breakfast. Or lunch, come to that.'

'So you hold on to those ropes as tight as you can,' said Bert. 'Because if you doesn't, then it'll be as our friend Mr Stinger here says. Sharks.'

Their interview with Bert at an end, the children were led off to their new jobs. In the galley, Lucy and Hermione met Mrs Bert, who was a large lady in a striped apron. She had false teeth, which she kept in a glass beside the pots, and whenever she wanted to taste anything, she would have to put her teeth in first. She was not unkind to the girls, and told them that if they worked hard she would give them a piece of cake at the end of the day.

Sam was taken by one of the pirates to the mast and told to climb up and tighten some of the ropes. It was hard work, and the pirate in charge kept shouting at him when he made a mistake, but what was worst of all was the way the ship rocked backwards and forwards. When he was out on one of the cross-spars that held the sail, he could find himself dipping down towards the water at an alarming rate, only to be tipped heavenwards again before he knew where he was.

At the end of the day, Mrs Bert gave the children their meal at a table in the galley. They were almost too tired to eat, and Lucy and Hermione were longing for the hammocks which they had been given in a little cabin off the galley. Sam had not even been given a hammock; he had been told to sleep under a table in the galley, and a blanket had been placed there for him.

'Do you think we'll be rescued?' asked Hermione. 'I can't bear the thought of being here for the rest of my life.'

'I don't know,' said Lucy. 'I'm worried about Captain Foster. Will anybody find him in time, or will Biscuit know how to save him again? What if Biscuit can't get into the wheelhouse – what then?'

Hermione could not answer these questions, and nor could Sam. He had fallen asleep in his chair, and it was left to the two girls to lift him up gently and put him down on his blanket on the floor.

CHAPTER 6

Stowaway

The children were all woken up at six o'clock the next morning and set to work. Lucy and Hermione were ordered to sweep out the galley and polish all the pots and pans. Sam was set to scrubbing the deck, a back-breaking job that seemed to go on for ever.

The pirates were delighted to have somebody

to do all this work for them, as they all seemed to be rather lazy. Bert sat in his cabin all day giving orders, Stinger walked around checking up that everybody was carrying out these orders, and the other four pirates, who were called Bill, Ed, Charlie and Tommy, liked nothing more than to

lounge about on deck, whittling at pieces of wood and spitting over the side of the railings.

They were a dreadful lot, thought Sam. Charlie had scars all over his face and arms – each of them from a different fight, he explained – and Tommy had a mouthful of blackened teeth and spiky stubble on his chin. This made him look as if he had swallowed a cactus, which wouldn't have surprised Sam, as the pirate was always eating whatever he could lay his hands on – sugar cane, licorice ropes and large pieces of fudge specially made for him by Mrs Bert. Bill and Ed did not look as bad as the other two, but they each had six or seven large gold rings in each ear, and this made them rattle when they walked.

Sam was allowed to take a break from his deck-scrubbing every now and then, especially when Stinger was down below and could not shout at him to work harder. It was while he was having one of these rests, leaning against a large coil of rope, that he heard the sound that made his heart leap. It was not exactly a bark, but it sounded rather like one.

Sam turned round sharply. The sound seemed to be coming from the middle of the coil of rope and when he stood up and looked into it, his heart gave a leap. It was Biscuit! Sam put a finger to his lips and told Biscuit to keep quiet. The little dog seemed to understand, as he stopped his whining and lay down quietly where he was.

'Stay there!' Sam whispered to him. 'Don't make a sound.'

Sam looked around him. Stinger was nowhere to be seen and the other pirates seemed quite uninterested in what he was doing. Charlie was sharpening a knife, whistling cheerfully as he did so, and Tommy was sitting contentedly at the prow, eating a large piece of cake.

Sam made his way back along the deck and peered in through the galley door.

It was dark inside, and it took his eyes a few minutes to get accustomed to the darkness, but when they did he saw Lucy and Hermione sitting at a table, each polishing a pan.

'Psst!' said Sam. 'Lucy! Psst!'

Lucy turned round and saw her brother at the door.

'It's all right,' she whispered. 'Mrs Bert's not here. You can come in.'

Sam ran into the galley and told the two girls what he had seen.

'But how did he get there?' asked Hermione. 'Did one of the pirates bring him?'

'No,' said Lucy. 'They just ignored him. I think that he must have jumped over on to their ship without their seeing him.'

'Well, what are we going to do?' asked Sam. 'If the pirates find him they might do something terrible. They might make him walk the plank or something like that.'

'We'll smuggle him into our cabin,' said

Lucy. 'They probably wouldn't find him there. Can you get him, Sam?'

Sam said he would try. He had an idea which he thought might work, and when he went back out on to the deck, the first thing he did was to walk over to one of the rails and look out to sea. After a while, he put his hand up to shade his eyes, as if he was trying to see something. Then, when he thought the time was right, he shouted out at the top of his lungs, 'Ship ahoy! Coming our way fast!'

The pirates all sprang to their feet when they heard this and rushed over to where Sam was standing.

'Where?' shouted Tommy. 'Where did you see this ship?'

'Over there,' said Sam, pointing into the distance. 'Over there! Look, I think that's its mast.'

'Can't see a thing,' snapped Charlie.

'The boy must have sharp eyesight,' said Tommy. 'Are you sure you saw a ship?'

'Yes,' said Sam. 'There it is! Can't you see it?'

'Go down and fetch Captain Bert,' said Tommy. 'Tell him there's a ship coming our way. We'll keep watch up here.'

Sam slipped away from the pirates, who were all peering off into the distance with such interest that they would never notice what he was doing. Returning to Biscuit's hiding place, he picked up the dog and ran back to the galley. Lucy and Hermione were still alone, and they took Biscuit from Sam and spirited him away to their cabin.

Sam now went down to Bert's cabin and knocked on the door. Bert's rough voice told him to enter, and when he went in, he found Bert and Stinger sitting round a table, drinking rum and playing cards.

'There's a ship coming our way,' said Sam, saluting Bert as he spoke. 'Mr Tommy said I was to warn you.'

Bert and Stinger dropped their cards and pushed Sam out of the way as they rushed up to the deck. There, after a ten minute search of the sea with the telescope that Bert had stolen from Captain Foster, the pirate captain shook his head.

'You were right to raise the alarm,' he said to Sam, patting him on the head. 'Even if it's been a false one. You's got the making of a pirate, so you have. You work hard and one day you'll get a full-time job in the pirate trade, won't he, Stinger?'

Stinger tried to smile, but it came out all wrong.

'Yes,' he said. 'As long as no sharks eat you before then, you'll probably grow up into a good pirate.'

With these encouraging words, the two pirates returned to their game of cards, and life on the pirate ship went back to normal. The children, though, were all thinking of one thing. If Biscuit was on board, then Captain Foster would have had nobody to help him. And that meant that he could still be tied to his chair, with his boat drifting hopelessly at sea. They would have to do something soon, as there was not much time.

CHAPTER 7

Lucy's Great Idea

The pirates were so pleased with all the hard
work which the children had done that day
that Bert agreed to let them stop early and
have some time together on the deck before
dinner. This was a mistake on Bert's part,
because this was their chance to discuss
what they could possibly do to get out of
their terrible plight.

'We could try to take one of the rowing boats,' said Sam. 'We could lower it over the side and row away in the dead of night.'

Lucy shook her head. 'Not a good idea,' she said. 'We're too far from land by now and we wouldn't stand a chance of getting anywhere.'

'We could put a bottle over the side with a message in it,' ventured Hermione. 'Somebody might pick it up and come to our rescue.'

Again Lucy had to pour cold water on the idea. 'It could be years before anybody found it,' she said. 'That would be far too late.'

They were silent for a moment. Then Lucy smiled.

'I'm beginning to get an idea,' she said. 'If you want to get the better of somebody, what do you do?'

She looked around for an answer, but nobody could think of anything to say.

'You think of their weak points,' said

Lucy. 'And what are the weak points of these pirates?'

'They're greedy,' said Sam. 'Especially Tommy.'

'Yes,' said Lucy. 'And did you see how those two with earrings ate – just like pigs? It's disgusting.'

'And they're lazy too,' said Hermione. 'That's why they're pirates, rather than having an honest job.'

'Precisely,' said Lucy. 'So we have a group of greedy, lazy pirates. At the moment, they're in control of the ship, but we want to take over. So what do we do?'

Again, neither of the others could think of an answer. So Lucy had to explain her idea to them. When she had done so, nobody spoke for a few moments. Then Hermione stood up and clapped her hands together.

'That is a brilliant idea,' she exclaimed. 'A wonderful, brilliant idea that is bound to work.'

'Yes,' said Sam, a little more hesitantly. 'Very clever.'

That evening, while the pirates were having their dinner, Lucy went up to their table and said that she had an announcement to make.

'Oh, yes?' sneered Stinger. 'What could you have to say that would possibly interest us?'

'Maybe they're going on strike,' said Tommy. 'Maybe they've had enough.'

'Oh ah?' said Ed. 'Well, if you don't like your job, you can always leave the ship. And we'll even provide a plank to help you on your way!'

The pirates all laughed at this joke, but Lucy did not mind.

'We wanted to do something for you,' she said.

The pirates became silent.

'Do something for us?' said Bert. 'Well, that's more like it, isn't it? What would this thing be?'

'We want to cook you some popcorn,' said
Lucy. 'You see, this boat is full of popcorn,
and we would like you to try just a little bit
of it. We come from the Popcorn Islands, as
you know, and nobody knows how to cook
popcorn as well as a Popcorn Islander.'

The pirates looked at one another. Greed:
they could hardly resist the thought of a

popcorn feast. And laziness: somebody else would be doing it for them.

'Well, I must say you children isn't too bad,' said Bert. 'Why don't you do that little thing for us. What do you say, men?'

The other pirates all nodded their agreement.

'Shall we do it for lunch tomorrow?' asked Lucy. 'If you wouldn't mind giving us the morning off work, we'll get everything ready.'

'Naturally,' said Bert. 'It's all in a good cause, of course. But you'll have to work twice as hard in the afternoon, mind you.'

Lucy left them to the rest of their dinner and went back to the others.

'It's working,' she said. 'They fell for it. Now all we have to do is get everything ready tomorrow morning.'

That night, as they lay in their hammocks – or on the galley floor, as the case may be – each of them thought of what was planned for the next day. It was a very daring plan, which might just work. Of course, if it didn't work . . . Well, that didn't bear thinking about.

The next morning Tommy accompanied the girls down into the hold of the pirate ship to get supplies of popcorn for the lunch.

'We'll need a whole sack,' said Lucy, pointing to a particularly large sack of popcorn on top of all the others.

Tommy was a bit unsure, but his natural greed soon overcame his doubts.

'I suppose that's all right,' he said, as he lifted the sack down on his broad shoulders and began to carry it to the galley. 'I must say I can't wait to taste some of this stuff. I hope it's as good as you say it is, otherwise we shall all be very cross indeed and we may be tempted to throw you to the sharks.'

Sam was waiting for them in the galley. They had it to themselves that morning, as Mrs Bert saw no reason to cook if there was going to be a popcorn feast for lunch. So the children did not even have to whisper as they made their preparations, and they were even able to bring Biscuit out of his hiding place to give him a chance to stretch his legs around the galley.

The first thing that they had to do was to move the cooking stove into the middle of the galley. This was not difficult, as the stove was on wheels, which could be locked into position once it was in the right place. Then, when the stove was ready, Sam and Lucy went off to the bathroom and carried back the large tin bath which the pirates used to wash in. This was given a good scrubbing and placed on top of the stove.

'Now all we have to do is to pour in the oil,' said Lucy. 'And then we can put the popcorn in.'

The children went to the galley cupboard and took out several large bottles of cooking oil. These were poured into the tin bath, where they made a greasy, golden pool.

'Now,' said Lucy. 'Let's pour in the popcorn.'

There's a very large amount of popcorn in a popcorn sack, and when they had finished, the tin bath was filled to the very brim with raw popcorn.

Lucy stood back and inspected their work.

'I think we're ready,' she said. 'Let's put Biscuit back in the cabin and then we can sit down and wait until lunchtime.'

There was only an hour or so to go before lunch, but it seemed to the children that the minutes were dragging by terribly slowly. Then at last the hands of the galley clock pointed to twelve o'clock and they knew that it was too late to back out.

CHAPTER 8

A Lot of Popcorn

The pirates did not need to be reminded of the treat in store for them. At precisely twelve o'clock Tommy was at the galley door, where his eyes fell hungrily on the large tub of unpopped popcorn.

'Oh my goodness!' he cried, rubbing his stomach in anticipation. 'This looks very interesting!'

The others arrived shortly afterwards. Mrs Bert was the last to sit down, as she had some difficulty finding her teeth. But at last they were found in one of the frying pans and everybody was ready. They were all in a very good mood and were clearly looking forward to their unusual lunch.

'Makes a change from your potatoes, Mrs Bert,' said Stinger.

Mrs Bert glared at him angrily. 'Nothing wrong with my potatoes, is there, Bert?'

Bert smiled. 'Nothing at all, my dear. But I must say that I does like a nice bit of popcorn now and then.'

Lucy stepped forward and clapped her hands.

'Ladies and gentlemen,' she began.

'Oh, that's a nice touch,' said Bert. 'They shows proper respect for their betters, these kids. I think it was a pretty good bit of work we did when we stealed . . . I mean when we *invited* these kids on board.'

Lucy waited until he had finished. Then

she continued 'To thank you for all your kindness to us, we have prepared a traditional Popcorn Island feast for you. All I have to do is to light the stove and then, in a few minutes you will have all the delicious popcorn you could possibly eat!'

'Get on with it, then,' said Bert impatiently. 'We're all waiting.'

Lucy stepped forward and lit the stove. Then the three children stood in the doorway and waited. The pirates all watched hungrily.

'I hope it doesn't take too long,' said Tommy. 'I didn't have a big breakfast this morning. I was saving myself for this.'

'Excuse me,' said Mrs Bert. 'I saw you eating like a horse. You had four fried eggs and eight slices of toast. I saw you, Tommy. You can't fool me. Can you, Bert?'

'No,' said Bert. 'You can't fool Mrs Bert. I've tried for years, but it's never worked. You can't fool her.'

While the pirates were arguing, the children were waiting for the first sounds of popping. Suddenly Sam nudged Lucy, and Lucy in turn nudged Hermione.

'It's started,' Lucy whispered. 'There it goes.'

It is a special feature of popcorn from the Popcorn Islands that it explodes with a particularly loud pop. This started to happen all of a sudden, and the pirates let out whoops of delight. As some of the popped corn started to come to the surface, it was grabbed by eager hands and stuffed into eager mouths.

'Oh, this is wonderful!' mumbled Tommy, as he put handfuls of popcorn into his mouth.

This brought grunts of agreement from other popcorn-filled mouths. But now, as more popcorn exploded, something quite extraordinary happened. So much popcorn started to go off, popping and cracking like a hundred little fireworks, that it flowed over the edge of the tin tub. The pirates thought this was very exciting, and they got down on their hands and knees to scoop the popcorn off the floor. But they could not do it quickly enough. More popcorn went off, and still more after that. The galley was now beginning to fill up with popping popcorn, surrounding the pirates and completely hemming them in.

'Help!' shouted Mrs Bert suddenly. 'Stop this popcorn! It's out of control!'

Nobody heeded her cries. The children certainly did not. They had now closed the galley door and were standing out on the deck, looking in through the window at the pirates. It was an unequal struggle they witnessed. No matter how hard the pirates tried to stand up and get out of the galley, they were forced back into their seats by exploding popcorn. It was like trying to swim in honey – quite impossible.

'It's worked!' shouted Hermione. 'They're trapped!'

It was now a simple matter for Lucy to turn the key in the galley door and lock the pirates in. They could do nothing to stop her, and they shouted and waved their fists angrily as they realised their plight.

'We'll get you!' shouted Stinger, from the middle of a great mound of popcorn which

had surrounded him. 'It'll be sharks for you!'

'Well it's popcorn for you!' shouted Sam in reply. 'And it serves you right too!'

It was one thing to trap all the pirates, but quite another to take control of the ship. They would now have to try to turn it round and sail right back, hoping to reach the place where they had last seen Captain Foster. This would not be easy, as none of them knew a great deal about sailing, and the pirate ship was quite a large one.

'You go up and start pulling on those ropes,' Lucy said to Sam. 'Hermione and I will . . .'

She stopped. While everybody had been sitting down to their popcorn feast, the ship had continued on its way. This meant that the pirates must have left somebody in charge of the ship – somebody who was not in the galley!

Lucy quickly looked through the galley window. The room was now almost completely full of popcorn, and so it was difficult to tell exactly who was there. There was Bert – or a bit of him – and there were Stinger and Charlie, up to their necks in popcorn, and that arm over there, waving and pounding away to no effect, looked like a part of Bill. And of course Tommy could be made out in another pile of popcorn, or at least his stomach could. But there was no sign of Ed.

Lucy turned to Hermione and began to tell her what she had discovered.

'Ed must be at the ship's wheel,' she said. 'We should have thought –'

She was interrupted by an angry shout. There at the other end of the deck, shaking his fist in their direction, was Ed.

'What's going on?' he shouted. 'Where's everybody? Why have you closed the galley door?'

The children stood stock-still. Ed was now running towards them and nobody had any idea what to do. It would be impossible for them to resist him, as the pirates, even if lazy, were all remarkably strong. Ed would quickly overpower them and release the others, and then . . .

Biscuit leapt out and stood in front of Ed, growling and barking as fiercely as he could. Ed stopped where he was and looked down at the plucky little dog.

'Get out of my way, you stupid little animal,' he snarled.

Biscuit did not take well to being talked to in this way, and he let out a low growl.

Ed now drew back a leg and aimed a hard kick in Biscuit's direction. With most dogs, that would have worked, but Biscuit, of course, moved sideways. Ed did not expect this, and suddenly found a determined little dog latched painfully on to his leg.

'Ow!' shouted Ed. 'Get your dog off!'

Sam now ran forward.

'Pull, Biscuit!' he shouted. 'Pull as hard as you can.'

Biscuit responded, and tugged ferociously

on the pirate's leg. For a moment it looked as if he would just not have the strength to do it, but then, quite slowly, Ed toppled over and landed with a crash on the deck. This gave Sam his chance. Seizing a coil of rope, he wrapped it round the dazed pirate and rolled him over and over, until he was completely tied up. Only then did Biscuit let go of Ed's leg.

Lucy and Hermione ran up to see that the hapless Ed was firmly secured. They were both experts in knots and they made quite sure that whatever Ed did, he would not be able to free himself.

Then they all looked at one another and smiled. The first stage of the plan had worked very well. They were very pleased with this, of course, but they all knew that a major test lay ahead.

CHAPTER 9

Sailing Homewards

Turning the ship round was not easy. With a sailing ship, you can't just turn the wheel and leave it at that – you have to allow the sails to fill with wind, and that is a fairly tricky piece of work. It is also quite dangerous. If you turn the wrong way, the ship can go right over on its side and capsize, and that's the end of the voyage.

Lucy took the wheel to begin with, while Hermione and Sam busied themselves with the sails. They had to prepare all the ropes and scurry up masts to make sure that the sails were all ready. Then, when Lucy gave the order, they had to pull hard on several ropes to bring the billowing sails under control.

When everything was ready, Lucy shouted out, 'Ready about!' and everybody sprang into action. For a few moments the great ship seemed to lose speed as she turned into the wind, then, when the wind caught the sails again, everything began to tilt in an alarming way.

'Pull away!' Lucy shouted. 'Haul in the sails!'

Sam and Hermione tugged and pulled for all their worth. At first it seemed as if they were getting nowhere, and the ship leaned further and further over. A few small waves came over the deck now, and lapped at their feet, but they did not let up. Slowly the sails came under control and the ship began to right itself.

'Well done!' shouted Lucy above the wind. 'Now let's keep her like that.'

They made good progress. There was a fresh wind behind them and the ship cut through the waves like a dolphin. Now that the sails were in the right position, Sam and Hermione had less to do, and they could sit on the deck, watching the blue ocean go by. Biscuit enjoyed the open air; he had been fed up with hiding in the cabin, and he was very happy to sit up on the prow, feeling the salt spray on his whiskers again.

Ed, of course, stayed exactly where he was, safely tied up on the deck, and in the galley the remaining pirates floundered hopelessly in their mounds of popcorn. Tommy had eaten quite a bit of it while he was trapped, and now had a well-deserved stomach ache. The others just passed their time in moaning and arguing about whose fault the whole thing was. Bert blamed

Stinger, and Stinger blamed Bert, saying that he was not quite so clever as he had thought he was. Mrs Bert blamed both of them, and Bill thought it could all be put down to Mrs Bert's allowing the children to use the galley in the first place.

'And now we'll all be going to jail,' moaned Bert. 'That's a terrible end to a great career in piracy!'

'And I hear the food's not very good in jail,' said Tommy. 'Dry bread and things like that.'

'Better than Mrs Bert's potatoes,' said Bill. 'I could never stand those potatoes, to tell the truth.'

'You ate enough of them!' shouted Mrs Bert, pushing a heap of popcorn away from her face. 'You never turned down second helpings.'

And so it went on: moan, moan, bicker, bicker.

They sailed all afternoon and into the night. There was a bright moon out, and they were perfectly able to see where they were going. Lucy handed over the helm to Hermione, and she in turn handed it over to Sam. So they all took turns in keeping the ship on course, all the way until morning.

By Lucy's calculations, they were now not too far away from the place where the pirates had first seized them. Sam was sent up to the crow's nest, the little basket up at the top of the highest mast, where he could sit and keep a lookout.

If he saw anything, he would shout out to the deck below and the ship could change course.

Sam's shout came about two hours after breakfast, which was some rather old ship's biscuit that they'd found in the hold. Lucy was at the helm and Hermione sitting on the deck below. They both heard Sam's call, though, and looked up to see he was pointing.

'There she is!' shouted Sam. 'I'm sure it's the popcorn ship.'

Lucy swung the wheel round and Hermione and Sam adjusted the sails. There was a better wind in that direction, and the ship shot forward like a rocket. Soon they were close enough to confirm that it was indeed the popcorn ship, and a few minutes after that they lowered the sails and glided slowly up to the drifting ship. Biscuit, seeing

his master's boat, was almost hysterical with excitement, and it was as much as the children could do to stop him from jumping overboard and swimming the last little distance. Then at last they were there, and they gently nudged up to the popcorn boat and tied their ship to its side.

Captain Foster was very tired, and very thirsty.

'Quick,' he said weakly, as they untied the rope around his chair. 'Get me some lemonade from the cupboard.'

He drank and drank, and then ate the ship's biscuit that they had saved for him.

'My goodness, I'm glad to see you,' he said. 'I had almost given up hope.'

As the captain recovered, they told him what had happened and revealed that the pirates were all safely tied or locked up on the ship next door.

'Well done,' said Captain Foster. 'Now all we have to do is to sail back to the island and tell them that all is well.' The last leg of the journey was not difficult. Hermione went on board the popcorn ship and Lucy and Sam stayed on the pirate ship. Biscuit, of course, stayed with his master, and kept a very close eye on him.

They sailed through the afternoon, and into the night. During the night, Lucy and Hermione flashed messages through the darkness to one another. This was very useful, as in this way Captain Foster was able to tell Lucy what to do.

'Captain Foster says you should pull your foresail in a bit,' flashed Hermione.

'Aye, aye!' Lucy flashed back.

And then, when they were nearing the island harbour, and it was still dark, Hermione was able to flash the detailed instructions on how to make their way through the tricky channels that marked the harbour entrance.

Flash, flash, she signalled, which meant 'Go a little bit to starboard.' Or, *double flash, flash, flash, half-flash*, which meant

'Captain Foster says you should look out for rocks on the port side.'

Lucy made no mistakes, and when she finally brought the pirate ship safely into the harbour, Captain Foster and Hermione let out a great cheer from the popcorn ship. Then they all tied up, and stepped out on to dry land.

'We're home,' said Lucy. 'I can hardly believe it, but we've made it.'

That morning, the news of what had happened spread round the island within minutes of sunrise. It also spread to the other, smaller islands, and soon people were flocking across by boat to see the captured pirate ship.

The children were terribly tired, but they were determined not to go to sleep just yet, and so they stayed down at the harbour to give their statements to the island policeman and to watch the pirates being arrested.

The pirates made a sorry spectacle. All of them, except for Ed, were covered in bits of popcorn and looked thoroughly miserable. The island policeman looked at them sternly, wrote their names in his notebook, and then put handcuffs on them to prevent them from running away.

'What will happen to them now?' Lucy asked Captain Foster.

'They'll go to jail,' said the captain. 'And they'll stay there until Christmas. Then, if they promise to give up piracy and take an honest job somewhere, they may be allowed to go free.'

And I'm happy to say, that is what they did. Every single one of them, including the dreadful Stinger, became very sorry for what they had done, and all of them got honest jobs and became decent citizens. Bert was given a job as captain of a pirate ship in a theme park (not a *real* pirate ship, of course), and Mrs Bert took a job making hot dogs for the visitors. Bill, Ed, Charlie and Tommy all got jobs in Hollywood as actors in pirate films, and indeed they became quite famous for this. But they never forgot their promise to be good, and in fact they gave quite a lot of money to build a home for old sailors.

And as for Stinger, well nobody thought he would ever succeed in keeping an honest job for long, but he did. He became a shark scarer at a famous beach. Whenever a shark was sighted getting too close to the swimmers, Stinger would go out in his little boat and then jump into the sea near the shark. At the sight of the dreadful Stinger, with his frightening face and his mean look, the shark would usually turn tail and flee. It was a job that suited Stinger perfectly, as he was always happy when snarling, and snarling at sharks is as snarly a job as anyone can imagine. Of course it was possible that one day he might meet a shark who wasn't frightened of him, but then that's another story, and no job can be perfect in all respects.

But what about the Popcorn Islands? Well, life there returned to normal, and Captain Foster continued to carry the popcorn off to market and the islanders continued to grow it. There was one change, though. At the trial of the pirates, which took place on a much bigger, more important island, the judge declared that under the law of piracy, a pirate ship belonged to the person who captured it!

'So,' said the judge, 'I now declare that the pirate ship currently lying in the harbour of the Popcorn Islands is the property for all time, and for ever hereafter and theretofore, and all the rest, of those three brave children, namely, to wit, those herewith described.'

Judges have a very grand way of speaking, and what he really meant to say was that the pirate ship now belonged to Lucy, Hermione and Sam.

They were delighted by this, and they spent a great deal of their spare time polishing the decks and making sure that everything was in good order. Then, when visitors arrived, which they did from time to time, they were given a marvellous tour of the islands by the three children on their pirate ship. And when he had his holidays, which he now always spent on the Popcorn Islands, Captain Foster would give sailing courses in the pirate ship for all the local children.

These were great fun. At the end of each day – after a busy sail in the great ship – the children would sit on the deck with Captain Foster, and Biscuit of course, and drink lemonade. Then popcorn would be served – crisp, delicious Popcorn Island popcorn – of which no one ever gets tired. And as the sun would sink over the horizon into the sea, Captain Foster and the children would often chat about their adventure with the popcorn pirates, and agree that it would make a wonderful story, if somebody ever cared to write it all down . . .